Unicorn Magic
Seek and Find

SIZZLE PRESS

Magic Is in the Air

Mystabella and the Shopkins from the Shimmery Unicorns Tribe are here, and they all have their heads in the clouds. Can you search for these Shopkins among the endless rainbows and the starlit skies?

Mystic Wishes

Watch all your dreams come true when you spend time with Mystic Wishes!

Rainbow Scent

This sweet-smelling Shopkin is as fresh as they come! She's always up for a pampering session at the spa.

Cornelia Ice Cream

This little Shopkin is a pro at keeping it cool. She loves to chill out with Team Unicorn.

Twinkle Cupcake

This charming little Shopkin is a real sweet talker. She's full of sugar and joy, and has a bit of magic in her step.

Mystabella

This sweet-tempered, singing sensation is on her way to superstardom. She's kind and caring, which is why the Shopkins love her!

Bling Unicorn Ring

Bling Unicorn Ring is a real fashionista. She's got stars in her eyes, and when it comes to her dreams, the sky's the limit.

Twilight Cloud

Twilight Cloud is a bit of a daydreamer. She's often in a world of her own, imagining a big pot of gold at the end of a rainbow!

3

Shopkins Social

The Shopkins are having a party and the guest list has gotten out of hand. Can you find the Shopkins lost in the crowd?

. . . .

Checklist

Use the stickers from the sticker sheet to check off the Shopkins once you find them.

Bonus Challenge
How many Kooky Cookies can you find?

5

Clued-Up Cupcake

Can you follow the clues below to find the real Twinkle Cupcake?

1. TWINKLE CUPCAKE HAS GREEN EYES.
2. TWINKLE CUPCAKE DOESN'T HAVE A BLUE HORN.
3. TWINKLE CUPCAKE HAS WHITE EARS.
4. TWINKLE CUPCAKE IS NOT HOLDING A STAR.

A   B

C   D   E

AWESOME!

Baffled Banana

Can you figure out which of these shadows really belongs to Buncho Bananas?

A   B   C

D   E

6

Connect the dots in the puzzle below to reveal a magical Shopkin!

DON'T GO DOTTY!

WISH

Rainbow Riot

The sky is full of rainbow roads and there seems to be a bit of a Shopkins traffic jam! Can you find the Shopkins on the list below?

· ·

Checklist

Use the stickers from the sticker sheet to check off the Shopkins once you find them.

8

Bonus Challenge
Can you spot Mystabella?

9

Cupcake Coloring

Mystabella and the Shopkins need to be brightened up! Can you color in the picture below?

Cookie Chaos

Kooky Cookie is missing some crumbs! Can you help her out by drawing the missing half of the picture?

COOL!

Hazy Halves

Can you find the matching half of each Shopkin?

A
B
1
C
D
2
3
4

Crowded Clouds

Mystabella and the Shopkins love cotton candy clouds. Can you find the Shopkins on your list below as they play in the sky?

Checklist

Use the stickers from the sticker sheet to check off the Shopkins once you find them.

Bonus Challenge

Which Shopkin from Team Unicorn is missing from this picture?

13

Shopkin Sudoku

Which Shopkin goes where in the grid? There can only be one of each Shopkin in every row and column.

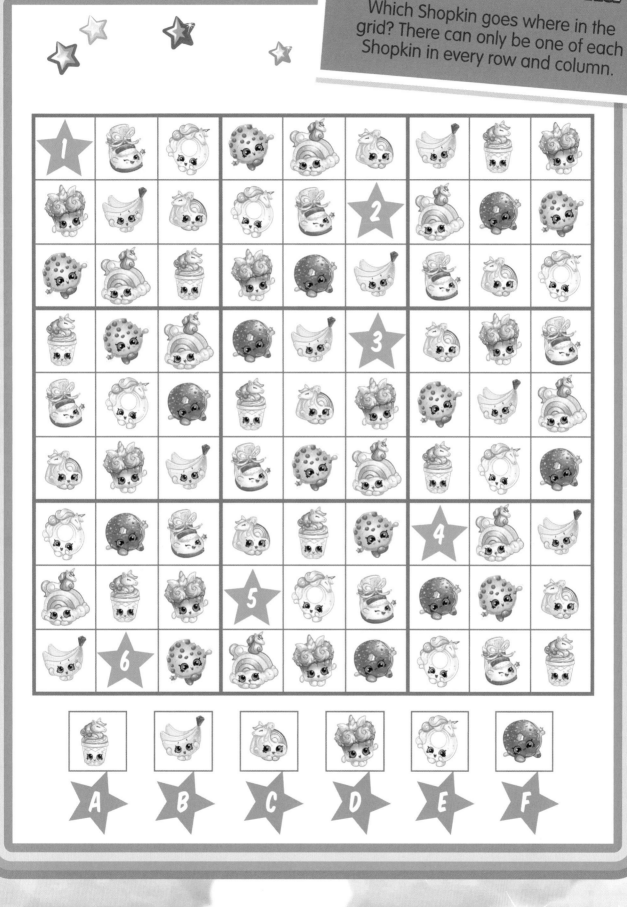

Starry Stack

The Shopkins are having a big slumber party under the stars. Can you find the Shopkins on the checklist?

Checklist

Use the stickers from the sticker sheet to check off the Shopkins once you find them.

Bonus Challenge

How many colored stars are in the clouds?

Stargaze Maze

Help Rainbow Scent, Lippy Lips, and Cornelia Ice Cream through the maze to find Mystabella.

Start

Finish

Glam Grid

Draw your own Shopkin by tracing and then coloring Bling Unicorn Ring in the grid below.

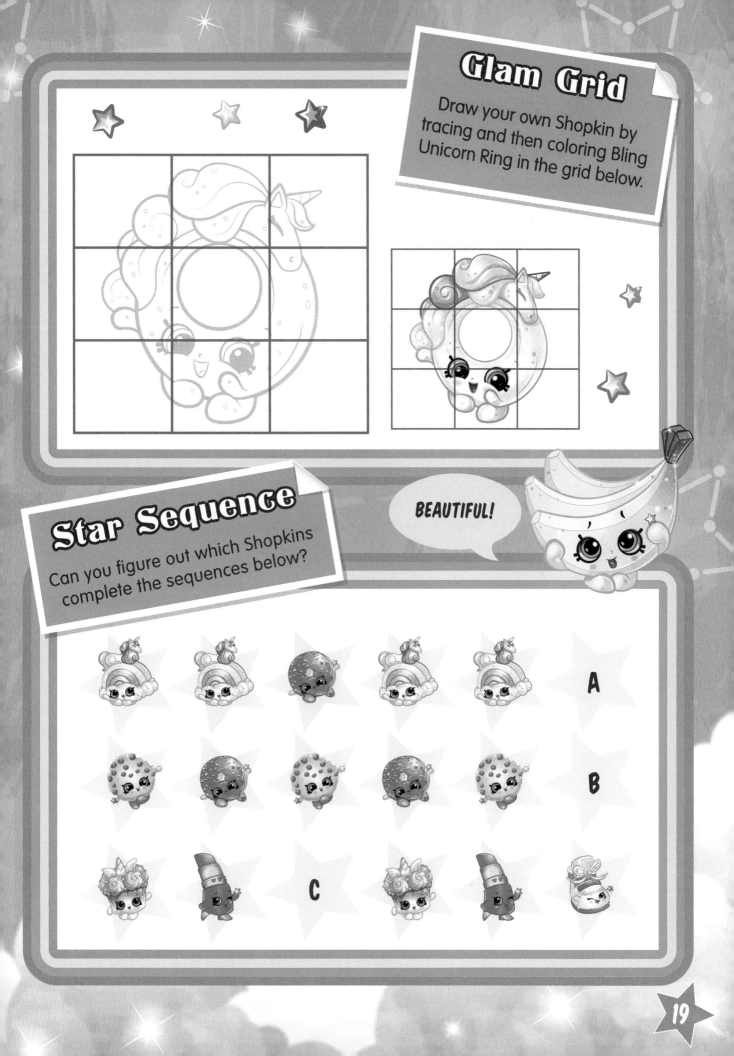

BEAUTIFUL!

Star Sequence

Can you figure out which Shopkins complete the sequences below?

A

B

C

Rainbow Ride

Mystabella and the Shopkins are playing on the rainbow slide. It's so popular, there's a huge line! Find the hidden Shopkins on the list below.

Checklist

Use the stickers from the sticker sheet to check off the Shopkins once you find them.

20

Bonus Challenge

How many Shopkins are on the rainbow slide?

21

Answers

Pages 4-5
Shopkins Social

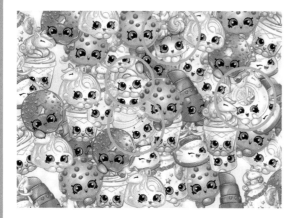

Bonus Challenge
7

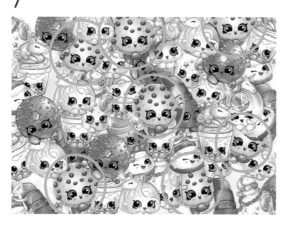

Page 6
Clued-Up Cupcake

A is the real Twinkle Cupcake.

Baffled Banana

D is Buncho Bananas's real shadow.

Pages 8-9
Rainbow Riot

Bonus Challenge

Page 11
Hazy Halves

A=3, B=4, C=2, D=1

HOW ARE
YOU DOING?

Pages 12-13
Crowded Clouds

Bonus Challenge

Twinkle Cupcake is missing from this picture.

Page 14
Spot the Difference

Page 15
Shopkin Sudoku

A=2, B=5, C=6, D=4, E=3, F=1

Pages 16-17
Starry Stack

Bonus Challenge
14

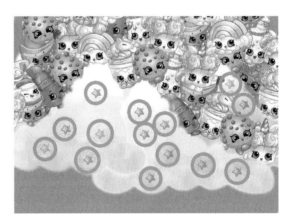

Answers

Page 18
Stargaze Maze

THANKS FOR PLAYING, SUPERSTAR!

Page 19
Star Sequence

A = , B = , C =

Pages 20-21
Rainbow Ride

Bonus Challenge
32